The Hideaway Deer

HOLLY WEBB

Illustrations by
JAMES BROWN

The Hideaway Deer

For George
HW

~

STRIPES PUBLISHING LIMITED
An imprint of the Little Tiger Group
1 Coda Studios
189 Munster Road,
London SW6 6AW

A paperback original
First published in Great Britain in 2019

ISBN: 978-1-78895-046-6

A CIP catalogue record for this book
is available from the British Library.

Printed and bound in the UK.

2 4 6 8 10 9 7 5 3 1

1

"It's beautiful," Lola said, looking up at the house. She set Alfie's cat basket down carefully on the weedy gravel and heard him mew crossly. He'd hated being shut up for the journey, even though it hadn't been that long.

"You really like it?" her mum asked anxiously. "I mean, I know we've seen it before but it seems different today. Now it's actually ours. Our house." She smiled and Lola saw her shoulders relax. Mum had looked worried and hunched up the whole time she'd been driving. It was as if the house was making her feel better.

"I love it," she said and leaned over to give her mum a hug. And it was sort of true. She would have a big new bedroom and there was the huge garden to explore. It really would be exploring too – the grass was so overgrown that Mum said they would need a map and a compass and maybe even satnav to get to the end of it. Plus the new house was really close to where Lola's uncle Chris lived.

It was only the things that came with moving house that Lola wasn't sure about. Leaving Dad behind for a start. She was going to stay with him for lots of the weekends, and that wasn't much less than when his flat was ten minutes away. But still – it was going to be so weird, not living in the same town any more.

The other big thing was starting a new school. Her old school was just too far to get to every day. Mum had sat her down and talked about it, when she found out she'd got her new job. It was perfect, she explained. She'd be working as a school receptionist, so she'd only be working during term time, and she'd be around to look after Lola in the holidays. There was a place for Lola at the same school too.

But Lola had been at her old school since Reception – she knew everyone, even the teachers. Now she was going to have to start all over again. Mum had said that Amie and Eloise, her two best friends, could come and stay, but that wasn't the same as seeing them every day at school. Who was she going to mess about with? Who would she talk to at lunch? Lola wasn't very good at talking to new people and each time she thought about it her stomach hurt. She was trying not to let Mum see how worried she was but she had a feeling her mum knew anyway.

Lola shook her hair out of her eyes. There were a few more days before school started and she wasn't going to think about it until then. That's what she kept telling herself anyway. "Do you think we can let Alfie out?" she asked. "He's so cross about being in the cat carrier."

Her mum nodded. "Let's get inside. He can have a quick explore before the removal men turn up, then we might have to shut him in one of the rooms. He'll need a bit of time to get used to the house before we let him out into the garden, just in case he decides to wander." She pulled the shiny new key out of her pocket and smiled excitedly at Lola as she put it into the door. Lola picked up Alfie's carrier and he butted his nose against the wire door, nudging at her fingers.

"You can come out in a minute," she promised. "You're going to love it here, Alfie. Did you see how big the garden is? It goes all round the house." She turned the cat carrier to let him see but he only stuck a clawed paw between the wires. He wanted to get out now.

"It's going to take a lot of clearing," her mum said, looking round at the long grass and overgrown bushes. "Still, Uncle Chris promised he'd help. He's coming over later on." She gave the front door a little push and stepped inside. Lola followed her.

It was a blazing-hot day for April, and the house felt beautifully cool after being outside. It smelled a little dry and dusty, as though the windows hadn't been opened for a long time – they probably hadn't. When they'd first looked round the house a few months before, the estate agent told them it had been empty for a while.

Lola put down Alfie's carrier and crouched next to it to undo the door. The black and white cat stepped out cautiously, his whiskers twitching. He rubbed his face against her knees while he eyed up his new home.

"We'll unpack your basket in a minute," Lola said. "It's in the car."

Alfie strolled away to investigate further, and Lola and Mum exchanged a relieved glance. At least Alfie didn't look too worried about moving house. Lola watched him peer into the living room, and then he marched into the kitchen and sat down on the floor. He glared meaningfully at Lola and she snorted with laughter. "Did you want a special new house second breakfast?"

"Actually, that's a good idea," Mum said, following Alfie into the kitchen. "We want him to think that the new house is somewhere he wants to stay."

"Extra meals are definitely going to help with that," Lola agreed. "I'll get the cat food and his bowls out of the car." She jogged back along the hallway and went to burrow through the bags and boxes piled up on the back seat of the car. She was just shutting the car door when a flicker of movement caught her eye – something in the bushes of the overgrown garden. Lola blinked and looked again but everything was still now.

"Probably another cat," she whispered to herself, hoping that didn't mean Alfie would get into a fight. As the garden was so big, their new neighbours weren't very close – there should be enough space for Alfie and any cats who already lived in the street. The garden backed on to an old cemetery as well, so there would be loads for Alfie to explore once he'd got used to the house.

She heard an engine rumbling down the road and peered around the car – the removal van was coming! Lola shifted the bag of cat food, which was slipping out of her arms, and hurried back inside.

"Mum! The removal van, I can see it!"

Her mum appeared at the front door, looking pleased. "They were quick! Can you go and feed Alfie and shut him in the kitchen?" She dropped a kiss on Lola's hair as she came out into the garden. "I know there's loads of unpacking to do but just think how nice it'll be to have all our things in the new house."

Lola nodded. She *was* looking forward to having all her stuff in her new room. But as she poured cat food into Alfie's bowl and he purred lovingly and nudged at her hand, that cold, worried feeling was still churning inside her.

The removal men had put the garden table and chairs from their old house by the side door from the kitchen, where there was a little paved area. Mum and Lola sat out there in the late-afternoon sun, worn out from shifting boxes, and watched Alfie stalking through the long grass. He hadn't approved of being shut in the kitchen and he'd darted out past Mum's legs while she was carrying a box of dishes. He didn't seem to be wandering too far, though.

"We should explore the rest of the garden," Mum suggested, but she didn't sound very enthusiastic about it. "There's a shed down there somewhere and a greenhouse."

"Where?" Lola peered at the jungly lawn. "I suppose they could be past that big tree." She stood up to look better. "Actually, I can see the greenhouse. And Mum, that tree – is there a ladder in it?"

Her mum frowned. "Yes, a rope ladder,

I think. Oh, Lola, is that a tree house?"

"I'm going to look!" Lola jumped up excitedly.

"Better not climb it until we've checked the ladder's still in one piece," Mum said, going after her. "I think we're going to need a bigger lawnmower," she added as they swished through the long grass.

"There's a football goal as well," Lola said, pointing further down the garden. She wasn't much good at football, but she quite fancied kicking a ball around this big lawn – once the grass was cut. Right now she'd just lose the ball.

"It's going to be an amazing garden," Mum said, tugging gently on the rope ladder to see if it was safe. "This feels OK, Lola. You can climb up it, but be careful when you reach the top. You need to make sure the floor's stable. It must be years old."

The tree house was old and weathered, and it was built right around the tree. They hadn't noticed it when they'd come to view the house – they'd been paying more attention to the house itself than the garden, and the tree house was half hidden by the branches, which were all just coming into leaf.

"This is a horse chestnut tree," Mum said. "I bet it has loads of conkers in the autumn. It's massive."

The trunk of the tree was so big that Lola was pretty sure that even she and Mum together wouldn't be able to reach all the way round it. There were thick wooden struts bolted on to the trunk to support the floor of the tree house – it looked quite solid. Lola heaved her elbows up on to it and pushed, trying to see if it wobbled. It didn't but she swung about on the ladder.

"It's OK," she called down as she heard Mum catch her breath. "It's just the ladder swinging. The floor doesn't even creak." She wriggled on to the platform and pushed open the door of the little house. "It's a bit spidery, though!"

The floor was covered in dead leaves and dirt but Lola could see how cosy the tree house could be once she swept it out. There were even some faded curtains at the window. It was surprisingly big too. Definitely room for a sleeping bag, Lola reckoned, if she wanted to camp out. Or maybe two sleeping bags, if she had a friend to stay. She thought of Amie and Eloise, and her stomach churned again. She gave herself a little shake. Maybe they could both sleep in the tree house with her when they visited? There would be room for three if they squashed up.

"I need to clear it out but it's great," she called down to her mum, popping her head out of the window. "And it doesn't shake about at all, I promise. You should come up – you can see the whole garden, if you look between the branches. I can even see a bit of the graveyard. Did you know the fence was broken? There's a big hole in it over there."

"Is it?"

Mum gave a sighing sort of laugh. "We'd better add that to the list of things to do. Come on down now, Lola. Uncle Chris is going to be here soon and he's bringing dinner. You could show him the tree house afterwards, if you like."

Dinner! Lola's stomach wriggled again, but with hunger this time. It seemed ages since their picnic lunch in the middle of all the boxes.

Uncle Chris arrived with a huge paper bag tucked under each arm, and then he tried to hug Mum and Lola while he was still carrying them and nearly dropped chips all over the floor. "Lola, I got you fish, is that OK?" he asked as they unpacked the fish and chips into the spaces between the piles of stuff on the kitchen table. "I wasn't sure, but I remembered you liked fish fingers at your gran's house."

Lola nodded shyly. She'd met Uncle Chris before of course, loads of times, but she hadn't seen him in a while. Not since Christmas, she realized, when they'd all gone to stay at her gran's. Somehow she'd never talked to him that much, although Mum had told her funny stories about all the animals he'd adopted when they were growing up. He was a vet now and he worked for a wildlife charity. It was one of the things that made Mum so happy about moving here, that she'd get to spend more time with her brother.

Lola watched as Alfie wound himself adoringly around Uncle Chris's legs. He never even did that to her and he was her cat!

Uncle Chris smiled. "Don't be jealous, Lola. It's only because he knows I'm the one with the fish."

"I-I'm not," Lola stammered, turning pink. She grabbed a stray chip to nibble on, to cover up that she was embarrassed, and listened to Mum and Uncle Chris joking with each other as they unpacked the food. Uncle Chris was one of those people who

could always make everyone laugh but it
made him a bit scary to talk to. Lola picked
at her fish, which she wasn't all that keen on,
but there was no way she was telling Uncle
Chris that. She could feed some of it to Alfie
when no one was looking...

A few days later, almost all the boxes were
gone. Lola's bedroom had new bookshelves
that she'd helped Mum put up, and her books
and little china animals were all unpacked.
Her new green and grey school uniform was
hanging in the wardrobe they'd brought with
them from the old house. Everything was
ready – except for Lola. If only they'd moved
house at the beginning of the Easter holidays,
instead of near the end. But it had taken ages

for the people who wanted to buy Lola and Mum's house to sell theirs, then it had all happened just in time. It seemed such a mad rush. If she'd had a bit longer to get used to the new house, maybe she wouldn't be so worried about school…

"That isn't true," Lola muttered to Alfie, who was curled up in a puddle of black and white fur at the end of her bed. "It wouldn't have made any difference if I'd been here since the holidays started. I'd still be panicking." She wriggled her feet out from under Alfie, and he rolled over and yawned and stretched. He opened one yellow-green eye and peered suspiciously at her, and then he went back to sleep. Cats didn't have to get up.

"Lola! Are you dressed?" Mum called from downstairs and Lola hopped out of bed.

"Yes!"

"Toast's on!"

Lola sighed. Mum was going to want her to eat a proper breakfast and she really didn't feel like it. She could manage juice, maybe, but at the thought of toast her throat seemed to close up.

She put on her uniform and grabbed her backpack, and then dawdled down the stairs. Alfie decided he'd had enough sleep and it was his breakfast time too. He lolloped after her, purring hopefully as they came into the kitchen.

"Oh, you look smart!" Mum smiled at her. "Sorry we have to go so early, sweetheart, but I've got to be there before all the children start arriving. Do you want me to plait your hair? We've got time if you want Dutch braids."

Lola nodded. She could plait her own hair
but it was much quicker if Mum did it. Dutch
braids would look nice for her first day. And
fussing about with her hair would use up the
time until they had to leave. She wondered
if Mum was nervous about her first day too.
Except it wasn't really the first day for her –
she had gone into school for a couple of days at
the end of last term, while Lola was staying at
her dad's. She'd told Lola the school was lovely
and so was her teacher.

"Here, eat this." Mum put a plate of toast
in front of her. "I'll do your hair while you're
eating."

Lola nibbled at the toast and felt the brush
tugging gently through her hair. She closed
her eyes as Mum started to plait, pulling the
long strands under each other. It was soothing,

feeling her mum's hands busy in her hair. "I could plait yours tonight," she murmured. Mum's hair was just as long as hers, dark and wavy, but she'd put it up in a bun for work.

"That would be nice." Mum leaned round to look at Lola. "It's going to be OK, you know."

"I didn't say it wasn't!" Lola said indignantly. "I didn't say anything!"

"Mmmm…" Mum tied a band round the end of Lola's second plait. "OK. Done. Stick your plate in the sink, sweetheart, we'd better go."

Lola got up and grabbed her bag, gave Alfie

a goodbye stroke, which he ignored entirely, and headed out to the car. Lola peered round the back of the house for a look at the horse chestnut tree and the tree house. She'd been up there a lot over the last few days. Mum had let her take the beanbag from her room, and she'd given Lola a faded set of picnic plates and cups to keep. It was like having two bedrooms, only the tree house one was secret and safe and special.

"Mum..."

"What is it, sweetie? Come on, we need to get going."

"Mum, *look*..."

There, just under her tree house, was a pale golden creature – and then another, leaning down to nibble on the grass, and another, and another.

The Hideaway Deer

"Deer!" Mum whispered. "Oh, Lola – aren't they beautiful!"

"We've got deer at the end of our garden?" Lola leaned against her mum, the weird churning feeling in her stomach forgotten. How could something so beautiful be in their own garden?

2

The deer felt like a good sign. Mum and Lola couldn't stop talking about them all the way to school – wondering whether they often came into the garden and where they slept and what kind of deer they were. Mum said she was pretty sure they were roe deer – she'd seen them at the rescue centre where Uncle Chris worked.

Mum and Lola were in the car park before Lola's wobbly tummy feeling came back.

"You can come and sit in the office with me for a bit," Mum suggested. "There won't be many people around yet."

Lola sat on a spare chair, listening to her mum answering the phone and chatting with the other receptionist, and thought how settled she sounded and how happy. As though she were in the right place. *Maybe I am too?* she wondered hopefully. But when her mum smiled at a friendly looking woman laden with bags and a bunch of plastic hockey sticks, Lola felt her heart suddenly thump inside her chest.

"Lola, this is Miss Addison – your Year Five teacher."

"Hi, Lola. Do you want to come along and see the classroom?" Miss Addison smiled at her, and Lola nodded shyly and came out into the corridor.

"Do you want me to take those?" she asked, catching the hockey sticks as they slid out of

Miss Addison's grip.

"Oh, thank you – I probably shouldn't have tried to bring everything in one go. Your mum said you were feeling a bit worried about moving schools?" She looked down at Lola over a bulging bag of books and Lola gaped back at her, caught off guard by the sudden change of subject.

"Um, a bit…" she murmured.

"It's a big change. But it's a friendly class – I'm sure you'll be fine." She nodded encouragingly at Lola.

"Anybody would be nervous. I'll show you the classroom and where you'll be sitting, and then I'll take you out to the playground and find a couple of the other girls to look after you."

"OK." Lola had to swallow hard to say it. She tried to remember the deer in the garden, the wonderful moment when she had first seen them. A day couldn't start like that and then go wrong. It just couldn't.

And it didn't. But it didn't go *right* either. It was just … fine. No one was mean to her. Everyone smiled and said hello, and the two girls Miss Addison asked to look after her were friendly. But Lola didn't belong. Everyone else in the class had been at the school for ages. They knew all about each other. Who had got lost in the museum on the school trip and who threw up on the Head's shoes in assembly and

That Thing That Had Happened in Year Two –
stuff that she would never be able to catch up on.

Those first couple of weeks of term, Lola
did her best to join in but everything she said
seemed to come out slightly wrong. She kept
on trying but it was such hard work having
to try all the time. It was so much easier not
to say anything. Just smile and wander off to
the library or the chess club or coding group.
Things where she didn't have to join in much.

It was OK – Lola loved reading and she
didn't mind being on her own most of the
time. At least, she didn't mind very much…
No one seemed to notice that she stayed in
the background and didn't talk, although
she knew Miss Addison was keeping an eye
on her in the playground – and probably
reporting back to Mum.

Mum kept gently suggesting that Lola should invite someone round but Lola just couldn't imagine it. None of the girls in her class were anything like Eloise or Amie. She said "mmm" and "maybe", and then tried to change the subject. But that wasn't going to hold Mum off forever.

Even though the deer hadn't been the magic good omen that Lola had hoped, she still loved them. They seemed to like the garden early in the morning and in the evening, just as the light was fading a little. They would come stepping delicately through the bramble bushes as the shadows began to lengthen.

If Lola finished her homework off fast (luckily Miss Addison didn't seem to believe in homework as much as her old teacher, Mrs

Lacey), she could scramble up the rope ladder
to the tree house and lie stretched out flat on
the platform. Lola kept so, so still that the deer
never knew she was there and she could watch
them till Mum called her for dinner. But as
soon as they heard Mum open the back door,
the deer would tense, their heads lifting – Lola
was sure she could even see their eyes widen.
And then they would melt away into the
evening, gone in moments.

Mum and Lola saw them in other places too,
not just the garden. They seemed to spend a lot
of time in the graveyard – which made sense
because it was very quiet and peaceful – but
they wandered all the way up the street and out
on to the main road as well.

Their new neighbour, Callie, came round to
say hello, and when Mum mentioned the deer

she heaved a huge sigh and explained that she thought she was going to have to give up having roses in her garden. She loved the deer, she said, but *they* loved her rose bushes. They jumped over her fence and nibbled the juicy growing shoots and the flower buds and there was just no point having roses, not unless she put them in some sort of deer-proof cage. She promised to give Mum a list of plants that deer didn't like very much, for when they did their garden.

They hadn't made that much of a start on it yet – there was so much to do in the house first. But one weekend in May, after they'd been in the house for about a month, Mum decided that they should go and buy a new lawnmower and cut the grass at last. The little mower they'd had for the tiny garden in their old house just wasn't going to cope.

"Can we keep the grass long around the horse chestnut tree?" Lola asked as she watched her mum plug in the new mower.

"Are you thinking about the deer?" Mum said. "Don't worry, I don't want them to stop coming into the garden, either. I'm not sure they'd mind if the grass was cut, though. It grows quickly, and they might even like it more when it's juicy and fresh. We can watch what they do. OK. Here we go."

Mum turned on the mower and started to push it through the long tangled grass. Lola watched – it was quite soothing, hearing the mower buzz and sniffing the sweet smell of cut grass. She sat down on one of the newly cut patches and tried to imagine what the garden would look like all tidy. She had a feeling it might be better a bit wild. But it would be good to be able to use the football goal.

Then the mower made a growling sort of yelp and Mum yelped too.

"What happened?" Lola asked, jumping up and dashing over as Mum turned the mower off and crouched down to look at it. "You didn't run over the wire, did you?" Dad had done that once; he'd said it was surprisingly easy to do.

"No… Oh … it's a stone. More like a rock. I hope it hasn't bent the blades." Mum peered worriedly at the mower. "I think it's OK. But could you do me a favour, Lola? Could you walk along in front of the mower and check for anything else like that? The grass is so long there could be who knows what in there."

Lola eyed the mower suspiciously.

"I won't run you over with it, I promise," Mum said, and then she crossed her fingers and grinned.

"If you run me over, you have to tell Miss Addison I was too injured to do that maths worksheet."

"Deal." Mum started up the mower again, and Lola grabbed a fallen branch from one of the trees and swished it through the grass in front of her. She found a couple of squishy footballs and a cross frog that she had to pick up and take to a safe spot in the bushes. She went on a bit more gently after she found the frog, carefully parting the grass in front of her with the stick in case any more of them jumped out at her.

There were no more frogs. But then Lola swept aside a thick clump of grass and stopped dead, staring. Just in front of her feet was a tiny creature gazing up at her with dark anxious eyes.

"What is it?" Mum called. "Another frog?"

Lola didn't answer – she hardly heard. The fawn wasn't moving – it was still curled in a tight ball in the grass, watching her. It was a rich golden-brown colour, the fur darkening almost to black along its back, and thickly dappled with white spots. Lola couldn't tear her eyes away.

The Hideaway Deer

There was a hush as Mum turned off the lawnmower and came to look. "Lola, what is it? Oh…"

Lola turned slowly, gazing around the garden. She was looking for the fawn's mother – it was so small, surely too small to have been left on its own. "Where's its mum?" she whispered. "I can't see any other deer. Can you?"

"I don't think so."

"Why did she leave her baby here all alone?" Lola asked worriedly. "It looks so scared."

"She could still be close by," Mum said thoughtfully. "You know how good their camouflage is."

They were right at the end of the garden, not far from the broken fence that divided it from the graveyard, and there were tangled clumps of brambles all around. The fawn's mother could be waiting anywhere, just out of sight.

"We'd better not disturb it – and the mum won't want to come back while we're here.

Let's go and get a drink," Mum suggested. "Can we see down this far from the kitchen window?"

Lola shook her head. "I don't think so. But maybe from my bedroom."

Mum started to roll the lawnmower back along the garden and Lola followed her. Then she darted back and laid her stick down a little way from the fawn's hiding place so they could tell where it was.

They dashed upstairs to sit on Lola's bed and watch for the mother deer to come back.

"Well done for putting the stick there," Mum murmured. "I wouldn't be able to see where the fawn was if you hadn't done that. It just melts into the grass."

"The mum's not coming," Lola said anxiously, kneeling up at the window.

"I thought she'd come as soon as we went away."

"Mmm, me too," Mum admitted. "I'm sure she'll show up soon."

But she didn't. They didn't see any other deer in the garden, just the tiny splotch of golden brown that was the fawn, alone and still by the bramble bushes. Lola felt herself twitching with nerves every time a bird fluttered around in the trees or a car growled by further up the street. But the fawn in the grass didn't move and no deer came.

"It's been an hour," Lola said at last, glancing down at her watch. "What if the fawn's been abandoned? Maybe something's happened to its mother?"

Mum gazed worriedly down at the garden for a moment more and then sat back, pulling her phone out of her pocket. "I'm going to call

Uncle Chris," she said. "He'll know what we ought to do."

Uncle Chris had already come over to watch the deer with Lola a few times. He loved them almost as much as she did and she was starting to find him a bit easier to talk to. He wouldn't go up in the tree house, though. At first he just said he was too heavy and he wasn't risking it. But then he'd looked at Lola swinging about on the ladder and shuddered. He didn't really like heights, he admitted, and the tree looked extremely high up. Somehow, being worried about heights made him seem a lot less scary.

"Hey. Have you got a minute, Chris? Lola and I just found a baby deer in the garden when I was cutting the grass... Mmm, curled up in the long grass at the end where all those brambles are... No, it looks fine – I mean,

I think it does. But there's no sign of the mum and it's been over an hour since we first spotted it. Should we be worried? We weren't sure if it had been abandoned, maybe."

Lola leaned closer to hear what Uncle Chris was saying and Mum put the phone on speaker for her.

"It might have been. But honestly, Molly, it's far more likely that the mum's just off looking for food and she thinks she's left her baby in a nice safe place. How was she to know you were finally going to get round to cutting the grass…"

"Hey!" Lola's mum laughed. "Don't be mean. You promised you'd help me! So you reckon the baby's OK? The mum will come back for her?"

"Deer do leave their babies for quite a long

time," Uncle Chris said reassuringly. "I'm pretty sure she'll be back any moment now. Don't worry, and I'll see you soon. Say hi to Lola for me."

"Bye, Uncle Chris," Lola leaned over to say, and Mum ended the call.

"See? It's OK," she said.

"Mmm. Can I keep watching for the mum, though?"

"Sure. But I've got to make dinner now. I can bring it up here when it's ready, if she still hasn't come?"

"Thanks, Mum." Lola hugged her and then went back to leaning on the windowsill, her chin propped on her hands. It was very peaceful, watching the quiet garden. She wondered how the little fawn was feeling. Was it worried about its mother coming back?

The Hideaway Deer

Would it tell her what had happened?

Lola sat up straighter, peering at the broken fence. Was that something moving? Yes – a delicately pointed face had appeared, ears twitching as the deer made sure that everything was safe. She slipped through, stepping round the bramble bushes and then nosing her baby in the grass. The fawn scrambled up on spindly legs and nudged eagerly at its mother, nuzzling at her belly to find the milk. The mother stood silently in the darkening garden as the baby fed – and Lola watched, smiling to herself.

3

"What shall we have for dinner?" Mum asked
as she parked the car in the drive. "It had better
be something quick." They'd gone straight
from school to Lola's Friday gymnastics class
and it was past six already. "We could have
pasta and tomato sauce. Or I could make a
tuna salad."

"Pasta, please," said Lola. "Hey – what's that
noise?" she added as she stepped out of the car.
She turned to look anxiously at Mum. "Is it
Alfie?"

"I don't know," her mum said, looking around.

"It doesn't sound like a cat. But I suppose if he was hurt… We'd better go and see."

"It's coming from the garden. Oh, Mum, maybe that fox came into the garden again! Uncle Chris said that sometimes foxes can hurt cats."

They had seen quite a lot of different animals in the garden as the evenings grew lighter. There was a fox that padded regularly in and out of the brambles, and they'd even spotted a badger hurrying around the side of the house. The hole in the fence seemed to be a highway for all sorts of wildlife.

"Alfie's far too sensible to go anywhere near a fox," Mum said. She was trying to be reassuring but Lola wasn't sure she actually believed what she was saying.

Then the cat flap in the kitchen door clicked and Alfie emerged with an indignant mew. He

liked his tea no later than half past four, and
that was pushing it. After six was just rude.

"Oh, you're OK!" Lola gasped, crouching down
to stroke him. "But what's that noise then?"

It actually sounded more like a baby than a
cat, Lola thought, as they hurried into the main
part of the garden. A loud angry wail, echoing
down the lawn.

"Maybe one of the deer's got stuck in the
fence," Lola's mum suggested and they sped up.

When they came level with the horse chestnut
tree, Lola put out a hand to grab Mum. There
was a deer there – but she wasn't stuck in the
fence. She was standing in the middle of the
grass. She'd obviously seen them – she looked
very anxious – but she wasn't running away.

The loud bawling noise erupted again and the
deer started to circle, looking panicked.

She clearly didn't want to be so close to Lola and Mum but something was stopping her from leaving.

Lola clutched her mum tighter. "Look – in the football net. It must be her baby. That's why she won't run."

"What's it doing?" Mum whispered. "Oh, it must have got itself caught up in there. Poor little thing."

The fawn bawled even louder. It could obviously see Mum and Lola, and it was terrified. It kicked and struggled but it was completely tangled up in the strings of the net. The mother kept darting round and round, the white underside of her tail flashing in the shadows. She was trying to work out how to free her baby, and stay away from Lola and Mum, all at the same time.

"It can't get out," Lola said. "Look – the net's all around its legs."

"I know," Mum agreed grimly. "And it can't keep twisting about like that. Its legs look so delicate – I'm sure it's going to get hurt."

"We could cut the net," Lola said, edging a little closer. "I bet we could, Mum. With the kitchen scissors. If we could get the fawn to keep still."

Mum shook her head. "I'm not sure, Lola. I don't want you getting too close."

"Mum, please…" Lola could see the fawn's eyes – it looked panicked. They were such shy creatures, usually they darted away as soon as they saw anyone. And now the little thing couldn't escape. She couldn't imagine how frightened it must be feeling.

"I suppose I could hold it still and you could do the cutting," Mum said slowly. "Would you be brave enough to do that, Lola? We might get hurt – the fawn is kicking, and I expect those little hooves are sharp."

"I don't care. I'll get the scissors." Lola raced back down the garden and grabbed the handle to the back door – then she realized that it was locked, of course. They hadn't even got in the house when they'd heard the noise. She had

to grab Mum's bag from the car and open the
front door.

She dashed into the kitchen, snatched up the
scissors, unlocked the back door, then ran back
to Mum. The fawn was still crying, sounding
more and more desperate now as it tugged
uselessly at the net.

"OK…" Mum took a deep breath. "If the
mother looks like she's going to attack us, Lola,
we'll have to stop and go back to the house. We
can call Uncle Chris for help." She hesitated.
"Maybe we should call him now anyway. He
might have a better way to do this."

Lola shook her head. "There's no time,
Mum. Look at the way it's thrashing about. It
could break a leg."

Mum sighed. "You're right. We've got to try
and do this ourselves – but if it's too difficult or

you get scared, we're stopping, OK? Ready?"

"Uh-huh."

They crept quietly towards the fawn, trying
not to make any sudden movements that would
frighten it even more. The mother flitted
towards them and then back again, uttering
shrill peeping cries. It sounded as though she
was begging her baby to hurry up and get out.

"Can you hold it still?" Lola asked, looking on
as Mum crouched down by the fawn.

"Ooof… Yes, but probably not for long, it's so
wriggly. See if you can cut the net."

Lola crouched down, trying to avoid the
flailing hooves as the baby squeaked with horror.
Its legs were thin but surprisingly strong – and
so was the net. It was a sort of plastic thread that
was really tough to cut through. Lola had to hack
at it with the scissors.

"Not much longer," she gasped to Mum finally. "That's the front legs free. I'm going round the other side to get at its back legs, OK?"

"Watch out for the mother," Mum said, still gripping the struggling baby. "She's circling around and she hates this. She doesn't know we're trying to help."

Lola stood up cautiously, keeping an eye on the mother deer as she hurried round the back of the net. The mother was plunging about the garden and it looked as though any minute now she was going to pluck up the courage to fling herself at Mum. Lola wasn't sure what she would do – whether she might bite or kick. She wasn't a fighting sort of animal – female roe deer didn't even have antlers to attack with. But Lola was pretty sure that she could manage a hefty kick if she tried.

She sawed hurriedly at the strands around the fawn's back legs. There wasn't going to be that much net left when she'd finished, she realized, but that was probably a good thing. Another deer might get itself tangled up.

"There!" She sat back on her heels. "I think it should be free now, Mum. You can let go."

Her mum stepped back carefully, pulling the net away from the fawn's legs.

The little creature jumped, legs flailing, and sprang away, staggering across the grass to its mother.

"Is it hurt?" Lola asked worriedly. The fawn
seemed so unsteady on its legs – she couldn't
tell if it was limping.

"I'm not sure," Mum said, "but I don't *think*
so. I suppose it's got pins and needles from
being stuck in a funny position all that time."

Lola nodded. The fawn and its mother
were nuzzling at each other. The mother deer
seemed to be checking that her baby was all in
one piece, just like her own mum would do if

she'd fallen over and hurt herself. She glanced back at Mum and caught her hand, squeezing it tight.

"Well done," Mum whispered. "I'm so glad we got the fawn out."

"And we didn't even have to get Uncle Chris to help," Lola whispered back. "We rescued the fawn all by ourselves. I wish we had a photo to show him. But there wasn't time to stop and think about photos."

Mum slipped her phone out of her pocket. "I might be able to get one now – oh no, they're going."

The fawn and its mother trotted away between the brambles, the fawn's spotted dark coat blending into the dappled sun and shadow. Lola sighed – some of the magic of the evening seemed to go with them.

"You know what?" Mum hugged her. "We need a treat. We can order pizza for dinner. We're far too heroic and clever to make pasta sauce."

"Oooh, yay. Can we have pineapple on it?" Lola leaned happily against her mum's shoulder. "Mum, do you think that was the same baby we saw before? It had really dark fur between the white spots – almost like black stripes."

"It could have been. But I suppose there must be quite a few babies around at this time of year?"

"I suppose…" Lola looked back at the bramble bushes. She was almost sure it had been the same one, with that dark dappled coat. Their own special fawn.

Miss Addison was a good teacher to have, in most ways. She didn't give out loads of homework. She liked singing and made everyone in the class do dance warm-ups before class started to get their brains in gear. She stopped work and read out loud for ten minutes at the end of every afternoon. All things that Lola liked.

The one thing Miss Addison did which Lola hated was news. She insisted on it every Monday morning. Half of the class had to get up and talk about something interesting that had happened over the weekend. The other half of the class did it the next week.

Lola had done it twice so far and she'd stumbled shyly through a description of painting her new bedroom and how she'd gone on the train on her own to stay with her dad for the weekend. She wasn't really sure – because she'd been staring at her feet while she did it – but she had the feeling that everyone had been yawning while she talked.

She just hadn't had any exciting news – not like Jackson on her table who'd apparently spotted a man shoplifting last weekend, and then deliberately tripped him up when the security guard was chasing him out of the shop. He'd *said* that the shop was giving his family a year's supply of ice cream as a reward. Miss Addison had said it was a very good story, even if she'd raised her eyebrows at the ice cream part and everyone had laughed.

But finally Lola actually had some news to tell. She was almost looking forward to standing up in front of the class. When Miss Addison asked if anyone had any exciting news to share, she put up her hand eagerly.

Miss Addison beamed at her. "Lola! Lovely – do you want to come up to the front?"

Lola swallowed a little nervously and pushed back her chair. She stood next to the whiteboard and gabbled, "On Friday night me and my mum rescued a baby deer."

"A deer?" Miss Addison leaned forward curiously. "That sounds interesting, Lola. What happened? Tell us nice and slowly."

"It was when I got home after gymnastics – we could hear a crying noise coming from the garden and we didn't know what it was. It was really loud. And when we went into the garden, there was a fawn all tangled up in an old football goal. Its legs were caught up in the net and it couldn't get out."

"What did you do?" one of the girls shouted out – Paige, she was called.

"I had to cut the net with the kitchen scissors," Lola explained. "But it was a bit scary because the fawn's mother was there. She was so worried, she kept jumping around and calling to her baby, and that just made it struggle even more."

"But you managed to get it free?" Miss Addison asked.

Lola nodded. "It was fine. It ran off to see its mum and then they both went through the hole in our fence. Our garden's next to the graveyard and the deer live in there a lot of the time."

Someone made a spooky "whooooo" noise and everyone giggled.

"Thank you, Lola, that was really exciting news to start with. Maybe you could write about the deer in your garden for one of our story tasks."

Lola sat down again, feeling that for once she'd actually done something quite special – instead of being that quiet girl in the corner of the classroom. Paige was smiling at her and trying to whisper something, but she was across the other side of the classroom, so Lola couldn't hear what she was trying to say.

Several of the girls in her class had been in the same dance recital over the weekend so they talked about that. Jackson had been to an aircraft museum this time and he'd brought in a book of paper aeroplanes as proof, after no one had been sure whether to believe his shoplifter story. News and their spelling test took up nearly all of the time until morning break.

Lola dithered between going to change her book at the school library or maybe just sitting outside. It was sunny. She could sit on a bench and read one of the books she'd already got out, she thought. She looked around for Paige, still wondering what she'd been trying to say, but Paige had disappeared out of the classroom as soon as the bell went.

Lola curled up on the bench in a patch of sun.

The Hideaway Deer

Before she had the chance to start her book, a group of girls from her class wandered over.

"Did you make that up about the deer?" one of them asked, gazing down at her.

"No…" Lola looked at her, surprised. Why would she make it up?

"I don't believe it really happened," the girl said firmly. "How could a deer get caught in a football net? The holes are huge."

"No, they're not…" Lola started to say, but one of the other girls interrupted her.

"Jessie's right. I bet you were just making it up to impress Miss Addison."

They all stared at her and Lola stared back, unsure what to say. She hadn't made it up. It was absolutely true. She shrugged a little. She couldn't make them believe her.

"You shouldn't lie," the first girl, Jessie, said, sounding a bit smug. "No one's ever going to believe you if you make up stupid stories like that. Are they, Ella?"

"Yeah." Ella giggled. "If you're going to tell lies, at least make them *good*."

"I wasn't lying!" Lola snapped. How dare

they say that? "We do have deer in our garden. I see them every day."

"Yeah, right," Jessie sneered. "Deer in your garden." And all the others giggled and smirked.

"I've seen deer round the graveyard," someone else put in, and Lola looked round to see Paige leaning over the back of the bench. "She isn't making it up. My mum showed me them once when we were driving past. There's loads. If she lives next door to the graveyard, then she probably does have deer in her garden. You don't know *everything*, Jessie."

"That's probably why Lola's so weird, living next to the graveyard," Jessie said gleefully. "Maybe she's a ghost. Or a vampire."

Paige rolled her eyes. "Don't be so stupid."

"Even if she does have deer in her garden,"

Ella said stubbornly, "I still don't believe the story about the football net. That bit was definitely made up." She looked round at the others for support and they all nodded.

"Definitely," Jessie agreed.

"I didn't make it up," Lola muttered crossly.

Paige folded her arms. "My mum works for a wildlife shelter," she said firmly. "And she told me about that happening. She had to go and help someone with a deer stuck in a net the other day, and she said it happens a lot. Anyway, if you're so bothered, Jessie, you can go and ask Lola's mum about it, can't you? She works in the office. Why don't you go and ask her if Lola's lying?"

Jessie looked unsure of herself for the first time. "She isn't going to say that, is she?" she muttered. "Not about her own daughter."

"So now you're calling my mum a liar as well?" Lola said angrily. She felt almost surprised that she was being so brave.

"No, she didn't," Ella protested.

"She did." Paige nodded. "Come on, Lola. Come and sit with us." She marched away, and Lola hurried after her to one of the picnic tables, where a couple of other girls in their class, Maisie and Hannah, were sitting. She could hear a hiss of hurried whispering break out behind her as Jessie and Ella and the others wondered if she was going to tell Miss Addison what they'd said.

"Thanks for sticking up for me," Lola said shyly as she and Paige sat down.

Paige shrugged. "Jessie's really mean sometimes. Ella and the others just follow her around. What was it like rescuing the fawn? Were you scared?"

"A bit," Lola admitted. "My mum was really worried the mother deer was going to attack us because she didn't understand that we were trying to help her baby."

"I wish I'd seen it," Maisie said. "Me and my dad saw a deer in the park once, but I've never seen a baby one."

"It was really cute." Lola looked over at Paige. "Which wildlife shelter does your mum work for? My uncle works at Abbots Valley."

"Same one." Paige nodded. "My mum takes me and my sister to help out sometimes."

"Uncle Chris said I could come and visit." Lola smiled at Paige. For the first time, it actually felt as though there was someone at school she wanted to be friends with.

"You should stay out of Jessie's way," Hannah put in. "You can sit with us at lunch, if you like."

"Thanks," Lola said shyly, wondering if, just maybe, things were going to get better.

That week was so different to the rest of the term so far. Lola had almost forgotten what it was like to have a group of friends to hang around with. She was careful – she didn't want to assume that she was always invited to sit with Paige and have Paige tell her to back off. But Paige and Maisie and Hannah didn't seem to mind. It was as if they actually quite liked having her around. They sat at their favourite picnic table at lunchtime on Tuesday, and Maisie kept making comments about Jackson and the rest of the boys playing football – comments that sounded like she knew what she was talking about.

"Do you play for a team?" Lola asked.

"Yeah, Woodside Wanderers. We're really good," Maisie said proudly. "Top of the league. Do you play football?"

Lola shook her head. "I like kicking a ball about but I don't go to a club. I do gymnastics competitions sometimes, though."

Paige sighed. "Great. Another one who's sports mad." Then she shook her head at Lola. "That doesn't mean stop talking!"

Lola blinked at her.

"You don't talk very much," Paige explained kindly. "You've said more to us today than you have since you arrived."

Maisie and Hannah nodded, and Lola felt herself turning scarlet. "Oh... I was just... It's weird, starting a new school."

"I'd hate it." Maisie shuddered.

"But now we know you do talk," Paige said. "So we're not letting you stop."

Lola smiled and felt the hard, scared lump that had been sitting inside her begin to melt.

"Are you OK?" Lola asked, looking worriedly at Paige, who was slumped on one of the playground benches. Lola had come in early with her mum as usual and she'd just wandered out to the playground to see if her new friends had arrived yet.

"Mmm."

"At least it's Friday," Lola said, trying to cheer her up.

"Yeah. Uuurgh, I'm so tired." Paige yawned hugely.

"What's the matter? Did you stay up late last

night?" Lola asked curiously. Paige was never normally sleepy at school.

"My mum got called out to an emergency," Paige explained, swallowing another massive yawn. "My dad was on a shift working late too so she had to wake us up and take us to my gran's house. We didn't get home till one in the morning."

"I don't think I'd have been able to get up," Lola said.

"Mum had to dress Immy this morning." Immy was Paige's little sister, who was in Reception, Lola remembered. "She was so tired that she didn't wake up until Mum had actually put her school dress on her. She was like a little doll."

"What was the emergency?" Lola asked.

"A deer. She'd been hit by a car." Paige sighed. "It was really sad. Someone found her by the side of the road and called the shelter."

"What happened to the deer?" Lola said worriedly, and Paige looked up at her.

"She died," Paige said at last. "Sorry, Lola. I know you love the deer in your garden. Mum said the deer died just after she got there. And it wasn't because Mum had to take us to Gran's first, I asked her that. The deer was just too badly hurt to survive, Mum said."

Lola shivered, thinking of the beautiful deer in her garden. She had seen them walking down the road – Mum had even had to swerve to avoid one that stepped out in front of the car on their way to school once. It would be all too easy for one to be hit. Her little fawn was so tiny and although the mother deer was a lot bigger, she was still small and fragile compared to a car.

"Where was it?" she asked. "Did your mum say? It – it wasn't near us?"

Paige sat up straighter, looking properly awake for the first time. The expression on her face made Lola feel cold inside. Paige's eyes had gone wide. "I-I didn't think," she stammered. "It was by the cemetery, but you said you lived on Coleman Road, and it wasn't anywhere near there. It was Gansey Street."

Lola shook her head. "I don't know where that is."

"The other side of the cemetery from you. That's why I didn't make the connection. It's a long way away, if you're going by the road."

"But the deer wouldn't be," Lola said slowly. "They'd walk straight through the graveyard. The same deer would come out on our road sometimes and Gansey Street sometimes."

"Yes," Paige agreed reluctantly. "But that doesn't mean it was one of your deer that was hit by the car."

"No. I know it doesn't." Lola sat down on the bench next to Paige. Her legs felt shaky. "But I can't help worrying. Did I tell you before how my mum and I found a baby deer when Mum was cutting the grass? It was curled up there all on its own and we didn't know anything about deer then so we thought it had been abandoned. We called Uncle Chris and he said it was probably just waiting for its mum to come back. They can't walk as far as their mums, you see." She swallowed hard. "I'm pretty sure it was the same fawn that got caught up in the football net. I could tell from the markings on its coat – I've seen a couple of other fawns and they don't have the same dark stripes."

She looked up at Paige. "What if something
really had happened to the fawn's mum – the
worst thing that could happen – and now it's
in our garden, waiting for her to come back?"
Lola shivered. "Even if it's not the same fawn,
I just hate thinking that there's a baby hidden
somewhere and wondering where its mother is."

Paige reached out and put an arm round
Lola's shoulders. "I know," she murmured.

"I didn't think of it before, I was just sad about the deer. I hadn't thought that she might have a baby waiting for her."

All that day, Lola kept thinking about the fawn and its mother. She could tell that Paige was worried too – they seemed to keep exchanging anxious glances across the classroom. Lola found it really hard to concentrate on her work. Luckily Hannah was in her group for Literacy. A couple of times she elbowed Lola to make her look as though she was paying attention when Miss Addison came round.

At the end of school, Lola and Paige dashed round to the office to find Lola's mum. She beamed at them – she was still getting used to seeing Lola with a new friend at school – but then her smile faded.

"What's the matter with you two?" she asked.

"Paige's mum works for the same shelter as Uncle Chris!" Lola burst out.

Lola's mum nodded. "I know, you told me the other day."

"Last night she got called out to an accident – a deer had been run over," Paige explained.

"Oh…" Lola's mum looked sympathetically at Paige. "That's so sad. Actually, your mum did call this morning to say that she was really sorry if you and Imogen were tired at school today because you'd had to go to your gran's last night."

Lola grabbed her mum's arm. "But Mum, what if it's *our* deer? The fawn's mum? Paige's mum got called out to Gansey Street and that's just on the other side of the cemetery."

Lola's mum frowned. "I think I know where that is. Yes, I suppose that's actually quite close – for the deer, anyway. Lola, don't look like that, love…"

"What about her baby?" Lola's voice shook. "Mum, can Paige come back to ours? I know I've got gymnastics, but can't I miss it for once? We could go and look for the fawn, just to make sure."

"Of course – if Paige's mum doesn't mind. I've got to be here about another half an hour, though. Paige, could your mum just pop in here to let me know it's OK? I can drop you home later, tell her."

Lola and Paige sped off to find her mum, who was waiting in the playground with Immy. As soon as Paige's little sister realized Paige was getting to go to someone's house, she started

begging to go too and then she went into a huge
sulk when she was told she couldn't. But Paige's
mum said yes, which was the important thing.

Both the girls paced around the reception
area outside the office, occasionally nipping
in to look hopefully at Lola's mum. Surely she
didn't need to stay much longer?

"OK! I've finished, I'm coming now," she said
at last. "Stop prowling about like that, girls,
please. Let's go and get the car."

Lola clenched her fingernails into her palms all the way home. The deer had been killed late last night so if she did have a baby, it would have been abandoned for hours already. She kept remembering the fawn and the mother deer in the garden, sniffing and nuzzling at each other after she and Mum had rescued the baby deer from the football net. They had been so beautiful, and so loving. She couldn't bear to think that the little fawn might have been left all alone. But if it was, then she and Paige had to find it. They just had to.

The girls jumped out of the car and dashed round the corner of the house into the garden. Then Lola caught Paige's arm. "We should slow down. We don't want to scare the fawn if it's there."

Paige nodded. "Sorry. I just hate the thought of it waiting…"

"Me too."

They crept down the garden towards the longer grass at the end, just past the tree house and the goal.

"Wow, you had to cut massive holes in it," Paige whispered, looking at the net.

"I didn't mind," Lola said. "Actually Mum said maybe we should cut away all of the net just in case it happens again." She pointed at the swathes of long grass. "That's where we found the fawn before, curled up in there."

"I can't see anything now." Paige crouched down to peer through the stems.

"I nearly poked the fawn with a stick last time. I was right on top of it before I noticed it was there." Lola swept her hand carefully through the grass. She was half hoping to see a dappled-brown back and half dreading it.

But there was nothing. No fawn curled up in the grass, even though they searched for ages.

"I don't think it's here," Lola said at last, standing up with a sigh. Her back was aching from stooping over. "Do you think we should look in the graveyard?"

"Are you allowed?" Paige asked. "Have you been in there before?"

"I went through the fence to look around once," Lola admitted. "Mum didn't say I couldn't."

"OK." Paige nodded. "There must be loads of places a fawn could hide in there. It's huge."

Lola led the way along the tiny deer-trodden path to the hole in the fence. "Watch the brambles! The graveyard is huge, but the grass is short. There's no overgrown bits like there are in our garden, I reckon that's why the deer like coming through the fence." She crouched down and pushed her way through the broken fence panel. Then she watched Paige scramble through after her.

"It's not as spooky as I thought it would be." Paige glanced around curiously.

"I know." Lola looked out at the long stretch of graves, gleaming palely in the spotted sunlight through the trees. "I think it would be really scary in the dark, though."

Paige sucked her teeth. "There could be a fawn hiding anywhere, Lola. This place is massive. All those tall statue things – there's loads of hiding places."

Lola sighed. "Mmm. Maybe. We should still look."

They started down the nearest pathway, darting here and there to peer behind the gravestones, but the only animals they saw were squirrels,

bouncing from tree to tree above them.
Then a faint rustle behind them made Lola
whirl round and clutch at Paige. "Look!" she
breathed.

Stepping slowly past them came a group of
deer, their ears flickering as they watched the
two girls inquisitively. They were all does, Lola
thought, with no antlers. They didn't seem
very scared – perhaps they were used to people
walking through the cemetery.

"They're beautiful!" Paige whispered.

Suddenly the deer scattered, bouncing wildly across the path and disappearing between the gravestones.

"What spooked them?" Paige asked, giggling in surprise. "Oh – is that your mum calling?"

"Lola! Paige! Where are you?"

Lola nodded and they raced back to the broken fence, quickly squeezing through and weaving between the bramble bushes. Lola's mum was standing just outside the kitchen door, holding a plate of sandwiches.

"Did you go through the fence?" she asked, frowning a little.

Lola looked at her apologetically. "We looked all through the grass in our garden and we couldn't see the fawn, and then we thought maybe in the cemetery…" She shifted uncomfortably. "We should have asked."

"Sorry," Paige murmured.

"You shouldn't go in there on your own," Mum said. "I didn't know where you were! Anyway, I was coming to help you look. But have some of these first."

"Thanks." Lola picked up a sandwich. She was actually quite hungry, as she hadn't eaten very much of her lunch. Paige took one as well and they ate silently, looking around the garden.

"If the deer left her baby somewhere in the cemetery, I don't think we'll ever find it," Lola said at last. "We saw some deer, Mum, and they just disappeared into all those bushes and trees. There could be lots and lots of fawns hidden in there. It's hopeless."

Mum put the rest of the sandwiches down on the grass and hugged her. "We can go back and keep looking," she said gently. "Perhaps if the baby really has been left alone for a while, it'll be calling for its mum. We might hear it."

Lola swallowed hard. She knew Mum was trying to help, but the idea of the fawn crying for its mother was so sad. She sniffed and then glanced at Paige. "We have to try?" she said hesitantly. Perhaps Paige was sick of looking. But Paige nodded firmly.

"We can't give up."

They searched for another hour but by then the sun was going down and the shadows were starting to grow thicker around the old cemetery. The fading light made the trees seem taller and there were strange, eerie patches of darkness around the graves. Paige and Lola found themselves walking closer together, and even Lola's mum was looking nervous.

"Paige, I promised your mum I'd have you

home soon," she said at last. "We've just got time for some more sandwiches. I'm sorry I haven't cooked you a proper tea."

"It doesn't matter – it was more important to keep looking." Paige sighed sadly. "The fawn could still be here and we'd never know."

"Don't say that." Lola shook her head miserably. "Maybe the deer your mum saw didn't have a baby."

"Maybe."

They walked back through the graveyard, hurrying a little past the deeper patches of shadow. Somehow, Lola thought as they stepped through the fence, her garden seemed brighter and sunnier than before. But perhaps the fawn was still out there in the deepening darkness, wondering why its mother hadn't come back.

6

The next morning, Lola woke early with a start. She hadn't slept that well. She'd kept having strange dreams where she was chasing something and couldn't catch it, and it was so terribly important but she didn't know why.

They must all have been about the fawn, she realized as Alfie yawned and stretched and padded his paws up and down on her feet. He obviously hadn't had any bad dreams. Lola wriggled her feet out from under him and got up to look through her bedroom window at the garden.

The Hideaway Deer

There were woodpigeons in the trees, making a low *roo-roo* sound, but nothing else was moving. There wasn't even a breeze and she couldn't hear a single car. It was the sort of morning for something magical to happen, Lola thought. All gold and green.

So why not look for the fawn again?

Her heart started to beat a little faster and she grabbed a sweater to throw on over her pyjamas. Mum was still asleep, she guessed, so she crept down the stairs with Alfie weaving excitedly around her, wanting his breakfast. She stopped in the kitchen just long enough to fill his bowl with cat biscuits and pull on her wellies. Then she opened the side door and slipped out into the morning.

It was cold that early and the grass was so wet that Lola left footprints. She slowed down

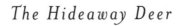

as she reached the big horse chestnut
tree but there were no deer staring back
at her. Lola eyed the patch of long grass.
Could they have missed a fawn hidden
in there last night? She and Paige had
looked so carefully.

She sighed, and a surprised squirrel
dashed across the grass in front of
her and scuttled up the tree. Lola
watched it disappear among the
leaves. Perhaps
she should just
go back in.

She was still trying to see where the squirrel had gone when she caught the tiniest movement out of the corner of her eye. Just a twitch, at the very edge of the long grass. In amongst the bramble bushes.

They hadn't looked there. The brambles were lethal, armed with long curved thorns. Lola had scratched her legs badly the first time she'd tried to follow the deer path through them to the fence. Surely they were too prickly and uncomfortable for the fawn to be hidden in there?

But as she watched, the purple-green bramble leaves at the very bottom of the bush fluttered again and a shining eye blinked at her between the thorny stems. In the shadows under the bush, the fawn was almost invisible.

"We walked right past you," Lola whispered,

crouching down to look. "You were there all
that time?"

The fawn gazed back at her, and then it
wriggled clumsily out from under the brambles
and stepped towards her on wobbly legs. Lola
stared – she had expected the fawn to stay curled
up and hidden, the way it had before, or perhaps
even to run away. She'd never thought that it
would come closer. It staggered forward
and opened its mouth
in a tiny cry.

"Oh…" Lola whispered as the fawn butted its head gently against her knees. "Oh, baby…"

The fawn looked up at her and cried again – a funny little squeaky noise. It wasn't nearly as loud as the barking wails that the fawn caught in the football net had made. This fawn – Lola still wasn't quite sure if it was the same one or not – sounded feeble and it definitely wasn't walking very well. Lola didn't know whether to be glad that she'd found it, or not…

"Have you been there since Thursday night?" Lola muttered. "You must be starving."

There was a faint sound behind her and the fawn skittered away a few shaky steps. Lola looked round to see her mum standing there, gazing at them wide-eyed.

"Is that…? You found…"

"I think so. But how can we know for

certain? What if its mum just left it here this morning while she went to graze? I mean, its mum *might* be the deer who was run over but how can we know for sure? What if we try to help and we're not helping at all, like Uncle Chris said…" Lola looked anxiously at her mum. "I was talking to him about the deer when he came over the other day. He said if people pick a fawn up and handle it then the fawn starts to smell like humans and its mother won't want it any more when she comes back."

"If this fawn does belong to the deer that Paige's mum went out to rescue," Mum said slowly, "then I suppose it must have been here all the time. It wouldn't move, would it? Not if this was where its mother left it?"

"I don't think so," Lola said. "Uncle Chris said they're really good at staying put. I didn't disturb it, Mum. It just got up and came over."

"I know, Lola, don't worry. This isn't your fault." Mum frowned. "You and Paige looked really carefully yesterday. Wouldn't you have seen the fawn if it was there?"

Lola tried to think back. "I'm not sure," she admitted. "We did search for ages, but we were looking in the grass because that's where I saw the fawn before. We didn't look through the brambles. If the fawn hadn't moved just now, I don't think I'd have noticed it this morning either. It was tucked right under the bush."

"So it could have been there yesterday. Oh, the poor thing…"

The fawn had staggered closer, and it was nudging at Lola's pyjamas and making those faint squeaky cries again.

"I think it's hungry," Lola said worriedly. "It's really wobbly, Mum. It didn't stagger as much as that when we got it out of the net, did it?"

Her mum looked at her in surprise. "How do you know it's the same one?"

Lola shrugged. "I'm not certain. But that fawn had really dark stripes on its back between the white spots, just like this one does. I'm *almost* sure it's the same. Mum, what should we do? If it hasn't had any food since Thursday night it must be so weak…"

"Let's wait a bit longer," Mum suggested. "Till lunchtime, say, just in case it does still have a mum looking after it. And I'll call Uncle Chris and see what he thinks."

"OK." Lola nodded. "So we leave the fawn then?"

"Just for a bit longer."

The Hideaway Deer

Lola swallowed and started to edge backwards towards the house. The fawn watched her and Mum for a moment, then it squeaked again and staggered through the grass after them.

"It's following us!" Lola whispered. "Mum, I think we need to call Uncle Chris *now*."

Mum nodded and they hurried back to
the house, leaving the fawn watching them,
bleating anxiously. Lola kept looking round
at it. She felt awful, seeing the poor baby
deer so miserable and probably hungry. But
if the fawn's mum had just left it under the
brambles that morning and she and Mum
made a big fuss over it, it might end up being
abandoned for no reason at all.

"Sorry," she murmured as she pulled the
kitchen door to. Then she peered out of the
window over the sink, watching as the fawn
stood in the middle of the grass, looking
around uncertainly.

"Uncle Chris isn't answering," Mum said.
"I suppose he could be driving. I'll leave
a message."

Mum tried to persuade Lola to eat some breakfast but she kept popping up to check out of the window again. The fawn stayed standing on the grass calling miserably and then at last it curled up again, tucked into a tiny ball. Lola ached to go out to it but she knew she mustn't.

"How long are we going to leave it there?" she asked, giving up and pushing away the bowl of cereal. It didn't feel fair, eating cereal when the fawn might be starving – and it had gone all soggy while she messed with it.

Mum went over to the window. "We said till lunchtime… I know it's horrible, Lola. I want to help too, but what if we do the wrong thing? I looked up abandoned fawns on my phone and all the wildlife websites say to leave them alone."

"It looks so weak," Lola muttered, coming to stand beside her. "I hate this, Mum."

The Hideaway Deer

"I'll try Uncle Chris again," Mum said.
But there was still no answer. She put on the
radio, but it didn't help. Lola went upstairs to
get dressed and when she looked out of her
bedroom window the fawn was still there. It
had its head resting on its hooves and its eyes
closed. It looked so small and helpless.

Lola didn't even try to do her homework.
She knew there wasn't any point – she'd end
up writing nonsense. She borrowed Mum's
laptop and looked up deer and how to look
after orphaned fawns instead. Mum was right.
All the websites warned that most "abandoned"
fawns weren't abandoned at all – they were
just waiting for their mums to come back from
grazing and feed them.

At last, after what seemed like days to Lola but
was really only a few hours, Mum's phone rang.

"Is it Uncle Chris?" Lola yelped and Mum nodded as she answered.

"Hello – no, don't worry, we guessed you were driving, or in the middle of an operation or something. Yes, it's still there, Chris. Curled up in the middle of the lawn." Mum paused to listen and Lola guessed her uncle was probably pointing out that the deer might not be abandoned at all. "Yes, but we know there was a deer hit by a car close to here on Thursday night and we can't help wondering if this is her fawn. It's looking so weak. OK… OK… See you then."

"He's coming?" Lola asked hopefully.

Mum nodded. "He says he'll be here in ten minutes."

7

Uncle Chris was carrying a big cardboard box and Lola peered at it curiously as she opened the front door for him.

"What's that?"

"Wait and see," her uncle told her, dumping it in the hallway. "Show me your fawn, Lola. Did you touch it?"

"No! I didn't want the fawn's mum to smell me on it and abandon it. You said that might happen. But I did get close, Uncle Chris, I couldn't help it. It came out from under the blackberry bushes and it followed me." She led him into the kitchen. "Look, you can see it out of the window. I'm really worried – I don't think it looks very well."

"Mmm." Uncle Chris leaned on the sink and gazed out of the window at the fawn. "So you reckon this fawn's mum was the one that was run over on the other side of the cemetery," he murmured. "It would make sense."

"Is there a way we can make sure?" Lola's mum asked. "We don't want to end up stealing a perfectly healthy fawn whose mum just happens to be off grazing."

"Not exactly." Uncle Chris sighed. "Look, you've done the right thing leaving the fawn alone. You're not going to like this but we may have to wait a while longer. Often the deer won't come back to their fawns until after dark."

"You mean *tonight*?" Lola squeaked. "But Uncle Chris, if the fawn does belong to the deer who was run over, it's already been alone since Thursday night – maybe even Thursday morning if that's when its mum left it. That's two days already!"

"How long can a fawn go without milk?" Mum asked.

"It depends how old it is," Uncle Chris

said thoughtfully. "Once a fawn's about three weeks old, its stomach starts to work properly – they're like cows, they've got four stomachs to help them feed on grass. So your fawn might be old enough to graze a little as well as feeding from its mum. But it'll still need milk too." He looked out of the window again. "Your fawn's lying on its side now. That's not a good sign – it should be curled up. And you said it followed you earlier, Lola?"

"Yes, and it was crying," Lola told him. "It sounded really upset."

"To be honest, those could just be the squeaky noises a fawn makes anyway," Uncle Chris explained. "But a healthy fawn wouldn't want to attract your attention. It would stay safe and hidden, waiting for its mum. If this fawn was crying and following you, it might well have been abandoned. We'd better go and have a look."

Uncle Chris opened the kitchen door quietly and headed out into the garden. Lola could tell he was trying to tiptoe so as not to scare the fawn but the little creature didn't seem to notice him approaching. It was lying on its side with its legs stretched out and its eyes closed. Lola thought it looked sick but she didn't know enough to be sure. Uncle Chris was frowning though and he looked worried.

He crouched down by the side of the fawn, motioning Lola and Mum to stay well back. Then he pulled a pair of plastic gloves out of his pocket, the kind that doctors wear, and put them on. Lola guessed he didn't want to leave his smell on the fawn. Uncle Chris reached out and gently pinched the fawn's skin between his thumb and forefinger, and pulled.

"What's he doing?" Lola mouthed to Mum, but Mum just shook her head. She didn't know either.

"She definitely hasn't fed for a while," Uncle Chris said. "I'm pretty sure you're right, Lola. This fawn doesn't have a mother."

"She? You can tell it's a girl?" Lola asked.

"Uh-huh."

"What are we going to do?" Mum said, coming a little closer. "Can we help? It's not too late, is it? Maybe we should have called the shelter and asked them to send someone else out. I just thought it would be easier to ask you…"

"I think we should be able to get her healthy again," Uncle Chris said slowly. "She's dehydrated. That's what I was doing when I pinched her skin, Lola. If it had sprung back straight away, it would mean she was fine. But it didn't go down, it stayed pinched up like a little tent. That means she needs to drink. And she's really cold – I can see her shivering. Have you got some old towels?"

Mum nodded. "I'll get them. Do you want to bring her in the house, Chris? Is that OK?"

"For the moment," Uncle Chris agreed. He reached down and scooped up the fawn in his arms. Her legs stuck out in all directions and she gave a tiny wriggle but that was all. Lola wondered if the fawn was just too tired and weak to struggle. She hurried after Uncle Chris as he carried the fawn into the kitchen and sat down at the table with it on his lap.

The little creature blinked around at the
kitchen and squeaked faintly. Lola watched,
biting her lip. It must be so frightening for
her – she had surely never been indoors before.
Everything must smell strange and wrong,
and there were great big people blundering
around. She wondered if the fawn remembered
the football net. It had only been a week ago.
Perhaps – just perhaps – she knew that Lola and
Mum were on her side? Lola really hoped so. At
least that might make this a tiny bit less scary.

Mum came in with the towels and Uncle
Chris wrapped one gently around the fawn.
"Can you bring in the box I left in the
hallway?" he asked Mum. "I brought some
bottles and milk replacement powder with me,
in case we needed them."

"Oh! I thought you'd take her back to the

shelter," Mum said, sounding surprised. "But
I suppose you need to feed her straight away."
She hurried out to the hallway and came back
with the box. "Is this the milk powder?" She
held up a tub.

"Yeah, but actually we need to start with
rehydration solution, not the milk. There's
some sachets in there, can you see? We need to
dilute it with warm water from the kettle? We
can try her on milk when she's taken this."

Lola spotted her mum giving Uncle Chris
a funny look but she made up the sachet and
passed him the bottle. Uncle Chris held it up
above the fawn's head and dribbled some liquid
on his fingertips. Then he smeared it gently on
her muzzle.

The fawn did nothing for a second or two and
then a slow pink tongue licked out, sweeping

around her mouth to catch the droplets. She
wriggled weakly and opened her eyes a little
more, clearly curious about the liquid. Uncle
Chris carefully lowered the bottle until the teat
touched her mouth and let her suck.

"We can't go straight to milk, you see," he
murmured. "She's lost a lot of minerals from
being dehydrated, that's what this stuff is
putting back." He watched the deer sucking
eagerly. "I'm glad she's taking it. Roe deer are
often really hard to feed – they're the most
difficult kind to hand-rear."

Lola nodded. The deer were so shy and secretive, hiding in the shadows of her garden. Every time she saw them, it felt like something special. It made sense that the baby would be frightened and might not want to feed.

"Sometimes they can take a couple of days to accept being fed from a bottle. But I suppose this baby's just desperately thirsty."

"Chris, why did you bring all this stuff here, instead of taking her back to the shelter?" Lola's mum asked, folding her arms and eyeing him sternly.

"Mmm. Well… We've got a bit of a problem," Uncle Chris explained, looking at Mum and then hurriedly back down to the fawn. "We're short-staffed. Run off our feet, really. And hand-rearing a deer is a tricky job. Especially a roe deer."

"A job which obviously needs to be done by an expert," Mum said grimly.

"Ye-eees. It's definitely good to have experience. But actually what's best is if it's the same person who does the feeding. One or two, anyway. At the moment, everyone at the shelter is so busy we're not going to be able to make sure the same staff are always working with the fawn. If we want to be able to release her back into the wild, she needs to have only a few people around. If she gets used to lots of people feeding her, she'll end up quite tame and that's not going to help her in the future. So…"

Lola looked between Mum and Uncle Chris, trying to work out what was going on. What was he saying? Then she got it. "You want us to look after her!" she gasped. "Really? Can we?"

"Maybe." Uncle Chris's eyes were still fixed on

the fawn. "We should think about it, at least."

"Chris, I work and Lola's at school!" Mum said. "How can we possibly hand-rear a fawn? Won't she need feeding every couple of hours?"

"No, no. She's too old for that. It's hard to know exactly but I reckon she's about eight weeks now. Old enough to need milk but grazing a little too. She's only going to need feeding maybe, oh, four times a day? Perhaps just three."

"That still means a feed in the middle of the day when we're both out," Mum said, shaking her head.

"Yes, but I could pop in and do that. If Lola does the other feeds, then there'll just be the two of us. It's a lot better than we'd manage at the shelter."

"Me?" Lola breathed.

"Yes." Uncle Chris glanced up quickly and

smiled at her. "I know how much you love the deer, Lola. You're always talking about them. Now you've got a chance to do something really special. But only if your mum says so, of course," he added hurriedly.

Lola's mum sighed. "If the shelter can't take her, of course we'll help," she said and then squeaked as Lola hugged her so hard all her breath went out. She coughed a bit and then went on, "But I'm worried about it. I mean, what if we do things wrong and she – well, if she doesn't survive? I don't want Lola to be upset, Chris. She's had a lot to deal with already over the last few weeks."

"Mum!" Lola stared at her. "I'm fine. What are you talking about?"

Mum rolled her eyes. "New home, new school, not living close to your dad any more, making new friends! It's a lot, Lola!"

"It doesn't mean you have to treat me like a baby," Lola pointed out. She was trying not to sound angry or upset – she needed to sound calm and grown up and sensible. "I understand that the fawn's ill, Mum. I know what might happen. I remember having to take Max to be put down, you know."

Max had been the beautiful ginger cat they'd had before Alfie. He'd been very old and his kidneys had failed. Dad had explained to Lola that it wasn't fair to keep Max alive with lots of medicines when he'd be feeling awful all the time. Lola had been really upset but she'd understood what Dad had meant.

The fawn was wriggling more in Uncle Chris's arms now, and she looked a lot less floppy and feeble. "Yes, you're a clever little girl, aren't you?" he murmured, rubbing her gently with the warm towel.

Alfie wandered into the kitchen and stopped dead as he caught sight of the fawn. He stared for a moment and then jumped on to the kitchen table. He wasn't really supposed to go up there but Mum and Lola weren't strict enough about stopping him and it was one of his favourite places to sit. He sat in the middle of the table and eyed the fawn suspiciously, and she stared back, ears flickering. Lola watched Alfie carefully, just in case he decided to go too close.

"I think she's definitely picking up," Uncle Chris said. "She wasn't alert enough to know what was going on around her a few minutes ago, was she? Molly, can you mix up some of the milk powder from that tub? It's replacement doe milk. We can mix it with the electrolyte drink, half and half this time." He smiled at Lola. "You're lucky. I think she's old enough to poo by herself."

"Whaat?" Lola stared at him. "What do you mean?"

"When they're very little, you have to rub their bottoms to make them poo and wee. Their mums do it by licking them."

"*That* is disgusting." Lola shuddered.

Uncle Chris laughed at her. "It gets worse. The mother deer then actually eats the – er – poo."

"No!"

"Yup. But for a good reason. It's to stop the baby's scent being spread around, so predators won't sniff them out."

"Please tell me we don't have to do anything like that," Mum muttered. "Alfie's litter tray is bad enough."

"No." Uncle Chris looked thoughtful. "But where are we going to keep her, Molly? She can't live in the house. Like I said, we don't want her getting really tame."

Mum frowned. "I hadn't thought… Um. The shed? It's only really got the lawnmower and a few garden tools in it. I could put those in the garage, since we usually leave the car out anyway."

"The shed? Not in the house?" Lola's face fell. "But … why? I thought she could live indoors with us."

"She's a wild animal, Lola," Uncle Chris said

gently. "You want her to grow up and go back to living by herself."

"I suppose," Lola murmured. She had been thinking how lovely it would be to have a fawn watching TV with her on the sofa, or sleeping at the end of her bed, but Uncle Chris was right. If the fawn lived with people, she'd lose all her wild instincts and she wouldn't be able to live as a wild deer when she was older.

"She needs to be able to go outside too. Would it be OK if I brought round some wire fencing and made her a little run?"

Lola's mum blinked. "Yes, I suppose. How long are we going to be looking after her for, Chris?"

Uncle Chris smiled at her hopefully. "A couple of months. At least. Maybe more like four months."

"Good thing we can't afford to go on holiday this summer," Mum muttered. Then she eyed Uncle Chris suspiciously. "You do know this is a one-off, don't you? We're not turning into the back-up wildlife sanctuary. If you start turning up with poorly foxes and sick hedgehogs, I'm sending them straight back again."

Uncle Chris nodded solemnly but he winked at Lola behind Mum's back.

Uncle Chris had explained that the fawn
needed to live somewhere that wasn't too cold
or draughty and said their old shed would be
fine. The fawn would be grown up and gone by
the time the weather got cold again.

For the time being, the fawn was curled
up on a pile of old blankets from the back
of Uncle Chris's car. He was going to come
back with a dog basket from the shelter, as
well as the posts and fencing. He promised
to teach Lola how to feed the fawn properly
too. Now that the little deer was feeling a bit

better, she needed to feed standing up the way she would if she was drinking milk from her mum.

Lola had cleaned the dusty window of the shed so that it was lighter and she and Mum could peep in without disturbing the fawn. Last time she'd checked, she looked as though she was asleep, snuggled into the pile of blankets. The shed seemed a bit gloomy and unfriendly to Lola but Uncle Chris had promised her that actually it was perfect. It had a boarded wooden floor, not too slippery for small hooves. He was going to bring back a bale of straw to spread out too, to make it more comfy.

When the posts and fence were up, they could leave the shed door open so that the fawn would be able to go outside during the day. She had to be able to graze and have some bare earth to nibble at, to make sure she was getting all the minerals she needed. So Uncle Chris said, anyway. Lola wasn't sure how that could be good for her.

Uncle Chris arrived back an hour or so later with a boot full of wire mesh fencing and fence posts, and a bag of concrete.

"It looks like you're building a prison camp!" Mum said, looking at the bundle of wire mesh.

Uncle Chris laughed. "This is nothing. If you actually wanted to stop deer getting into your garden, you'd need a fence that was two and a half metres tall, at least. Deer can jump over anything lower than that. This is just to keep the fawn in while she's little. Once she's older and she's able to look after herself a bit better, we can leave the gate open and then it'll be up to her when she goes back to the wild."

Mum and Lola helped Uncle Chris dig the holes for the fence posts, which took ages. Next they had to stick the wooden posts in the holes, then fill the space around them with concrete dust and pour water on it to make it set.

"We'll put it back exactly like it was, I promise," Uncle Chris told Mum, but Mum didn't look as though she believed him. She'd told Lola before that when they were growing up Uncle Chris was always trying to smuggle animals into the house. He'd left a pet grass snake sleeping in Mum's sock drawer once, because he said he couldn't find anywhere else to keep it. Lola reckoned Mum was right – Uncle Chris was definitely planning to send some more animals their way.

It sounded perfect to Lola.

They were testing the new gate that Uncle

The Hideaway Deer

Chris had brought along strapped to the roof bars on his car, swinging it gently back and forth to make sure it didn't get stuck, when Lola said, "Can we name her, Uncle Chris?"

Her uncle swung the gate again and looked at her thoughtfully. "I suppose so. As long as it doesn't make it harder to think of her as a wild creature. You can't fall too much in love with her, Lola. She's not staying forever."

"I know that!"

"It's easy to say. I've done it myself, especially if it's a baby you're hand-rearing. It's very hard *not* to get attached to them."

"I know she has to go back," Lola said firmly. "But I don't like calling her 'the fawn' or 'the deer' all the time. I want her to have a name."

"Mmmm, I see what you mean," Uncle Chris agreed. "So what are you thinking of calling her?"

"What about Dapple?" Lola suggested. "Because of the pattern on her back. I recognized it when I saw her this morning – it's what made me so sure she's the same fawn who was caught in the net."

"All roe deer fawns have spots, though," Uncle Chris said.

"Not like hers. She's got gorgeous dark stripes and white spots. I think Dapple would be a perfect name for her."

Uncle Chris nodded. "OK. It's a good name. Just remember what I said, Lola, please."

"I will." Lola sighed happily. "I can't wait to

show Paige all this. She came and helped me look
for Dapple yesterday, did Mum tell you? We spent
ages searching the long grass for her, and she was
there under the blackberry bushes the whole time.
Paige is going to be so happy we found her!"

Uncle Chris latched the gate shut and turned
to look at her. "Sorry, Lola. You can't invite your
friends round to see her. I know it seems mean
but it's the same reason we're making her sleep
outside in the shed and not in the house. We
don't want her to get used to people. The more
humans she gets to know, the less likely she is to
settle back into the wild."

"Oh…" Lola nodded slowly. She did
understand – but it seemed unfair on Paige, after
she'd worked so hard to look for the fawn.

"And to be honest, apart from the times when
you're feeding her, you need to try to avoid

touching her or even being around her too much. I know it sounds horrible but we need her to be frightened of humans."

"But – but why?"

"So that when she's grown up, she doesn't see someone walking through the cemetery and decide to go to them for food. Someone with a dog maybe or someone who's scared and reacts badly." Uncle Chris put his arm round Lola's shoulders. "Are you changing your mind about this?" he asked gently.

"No… I mean, I wish I could play with her a bit. But I know you're right." Lola sighed. "I'm just not sure what I'm going to say to Paige. She'll be so excited to know that we found Dapple. How am I going to tell her that I'm looking after a fawn, but she can't come and see her?"

"I understand what you mean." Uncle Chris looked thoughtful. "Maybe you shouldn't mention it to her at all? That might be easier than telling her she can't come round."

"I suppose…" Lola sighed. She'd been hoping that she could invite Paige to her house again soon. It had been so nice having people to talk to at school this last week. She hadn't really been able to enjoy having Paige over on Friday afternoon – it wasn't as if they'd had much time to talk. But she'd loved it that she had a friend she could ask for help.

Uncle Chris was probably right, though. She really wanted to do the best she could to look after Dapple. That was the most important thing now.

"There. Finished, I think." Uncle Chris looked proudly at the little fenced enclosure and the gate. "Now we just need to let her come out and explore while we put down some straw for her."

"Shall I open the shed door?" Lola asked hopefully.

"Let me just get in and shut the gate. Yes – go ahead."

Lola carefully unlatched the door and peered round it. The fawn was curled on the blankets still but she was wide awake and watching, her eyes gleaming in the shadowy dimness of the shed.

The Hideaway Deer

"Look..." Lola whispered. "There's lot of space for you now." She glanced back at Uncle Chris. "What shall we do? I don't want to scare her by going in."

He shook his head. "No, let's not. We'll just wait out here and see if she decides to come and explore. Then we can take this basket inside and put down the straw."

They sat together on the straw bale, watching but trying not to make themselves too obvious. Lola leaned forward with her chin on her hands, feeling sleepy. She hadn't slept well the night before and she'd got up so early. She could feel her eyes closing.

Then someone dug her gently in the ribs and she sat up. "Look," Uncle Chris murmured in her ear.

The fawn was at the door of the shed,

looking cautiously out into the garden. She
could obviously see Lola and Uncle Chris –
she kept darting careful little looks at them.
But in the end she seemed to decide that they
were mostly harmless. She stepped delicately
out of the doorway and into the enclosure.
Then she went sniffing and nosing around the
edge of the fence, stopping every so often for a
nibble of grass.

Uncle Chris stood up, moving very slowly so as not to spook Dapple, and picked up the straw bale. He carried it into the shed, slit the bindings and started to scatter straw around the floor. Lola brought in the basket and put one of the old blankets inside it for a cushion, fluffing it up to make it look comfy. Then she laughed. The fawn was standing at the door of the shed now, eyeing them curiously.

"Nice new bed," Lola whispered to her. Then she wondered if she shouldn't have said it. Did that count as being too friendly and encouraging Dapple to get too tame?

She sighed. This was going to be so much harder than she'd thought.

For the next few days, Dapple drank her bottles eagerly and spent the day pattering around her little yard, snuffling for daisies and dandelions in the grass. Lola fed her early in the morning – usually in her pyjamas, so as not to get her school uniform mucky – and then once when she'd got home from school and once just before bed. Uncle Chris popped in from work to feed the fawn at lunchtime.

Lola was pretty sure that she could *see* Dapple growing. The little deer seemed to become plumper and glossier every day. Her white spots glowed in the dark of the shed when she bounced up to greet Lola coming with her bottle.

It was hard for Lola not to pet the fawn, like she would with Alfie. Dapple's coat looked so shiny and soft and she nuzzled so hopefully at Lola's fingers when Lola was too slow with the milk.

But it was even harder not to tell Paige – and
Hannah and Maisie and Miss Addison and
everyone else in the class – about her. Lola
was desperate to share the news. Paige and
the others had been so interested in her story
about freeing Dapple from the football net.
She knew they'd love to hear that Dapple was
living in her garden shed now. Paige had even
hugged her on that first Monday morning and
said she was sorry that they hadn't found the
fawn. Lola had felt like the world's biggest liar.
She'd almost burst out, "But I did!" And then
she remembered what Uncle Chris had said
and clamped her mouth shut.

As the weeks went on, and Dapple grew
bigger and healthier and even more beautiful,
Lola hated not being able to tell her new
friend what she was doing.

Luckily, Paige was distracted from thinking about the fawn. Her birthday was just before school broke up for summer and her mum had promised her a sleepover party on the last day. Paige had been planning it ever since half-term, but now her birthday was only a few days away, and she couldn't stop talking about it – what sort of birthday cake she ought to have and what films they should watch and how her mum wouldn't mind if they stayed up really, really late. Lola had been so excited when Paige gave her the invitation the week before – she was starting to feel like she actually belonged.

When Paige came running towards her in the playground one morning a couple of days before the party, Lola thought it was to tell her more party news. That maybe her mum had agreed to getting pizzas delivered after all. But it wasn't.

"Why didn't you tell me?" Paige demanded, standing right in front of Lola and staring at her. She looked so hurt.

"Wh-what?" Lola stammered, her heart suddenly thumping. Maisie and Hannah were watching, whispering together worriedly.

"About the fawn! After all that time we spent looking for her, how could you not tell me that you found her? I thought we were friends!"

"We are!" Lola gasped. "Paige, we are friends. I couldn't tell you, that was all. I couldn't tell anyone. How do you even know?"

"Your uncle told my mum and she told me! Actually, she didn't tell me. She asked was it going to be OK you coming to my sleepover when you had to feed your fawn four times a day? Like I already knew about it!"

"Oh…" Lola stared at her feet. She felt awful. The ends of her fingers had gone all cold.

"So why didn't you tell me?" Paige shook her head. "I'm not sure I even want to know. Lola, you lied to me! You said you never found her!"

"I didn't," Lola whispered. Because she had tried so very hard not to tell Paige that. She'd just nodded and looked sad. But she *had* deliberately let her friend think they hadn't found Dapple when she'd asked and that was just as bad.

She looked up at Paige, twisting her fingers. "Uncle Chris said not to tell you – not to tell anyone from school. Because then you'd want to come and see her and she's not supposed to get used to any more people than just me and him. She mustn't get tame, don't you see? We want to release her back into the wild when she's big enough."

"So? You could have just told me that," Paige said, and Lola was sure that she was almost crying. "I'm not stupid, Lola. I'd have understood!"

"I know," Lola muttered. "I should have told you. I was the one being stupid. I'm really sorry." Now Paige said it, Lola could see that she was right. Why hadn't she just explained about Dapple having to stay scared of people? If Lola could understand it, why wouldn't Paige and the others? Uncle Chris had meant well but he'd been absolutely wrong. Even if

Paige had begged to come and see Dapple and
Lola had to say no, it wouldn't have been as
bad as this.

"I was just trying to do the right thing," she
whispered. "I'm sorry, Paige."

"I can't believe you didn't trust me." Paige
really was crying now, which only made Lola
feel worse. "You're supposed to be coming to
my party!"

Lola stared at her miserably. "Do you – do
you not want me to come any more?"

Paige just stood there, sniffing back tears.

"I don't know…" she whispered.

9

Lola just about managed not to cry at school. She spent break and lunchtime hiding in the library, trying to pretend she was fine. But she wasn't. Everybody else in their class seemed to know that she and Paige had had a fight – whenever she walked past, there was a little hissing tide of whispers. And in Numeracy, when they were supposed to be talking about decimals, Jessie was smirking and gossiping, telling everyone that, "Lola's been so horrible to poor Paige…"

At the end of the day Lola trailed into the office. Her mum smiled at her – and that was it.

Lola stopped trying not to cry and leaned against Mum, her shoulders shaking.

"What happened?" Mum asked, trying to get Lola to look at her. "Lola, what's the matter?"

Mum listened as Lola sniffed and sobbed her way through the explanation.

"I wish you'd said." Mum sighed. "We could've arranged for Paige to come over and just look at Dapple from the other side of the garden or something like that. She's sensible. She wouldn't have minded."

"I know that now," Lola wailed. "But Uncle Chris said and he knows about animals so I did what he told me! And now Paige won't even talk to me!"

"Oh, love." Lola's mum looked at her worriedly. "The party? Isn't it the day after tomorrow? The last day of term?"

Lola shook her head. "I'm not going to go.

I can't. Just tell Paige's mum I'm not well or something." She rubbed her eyes wearily. "Please can we go home?"

Mum offered to feed Dapple for Lola that afternoon, or call Uncle Chris and ask him to do it – she said this was partly his fault, so he ought to come and make up for it. But Lola just sniffed and shook her head. It wasn't fair on Dapple to change things around like that – she didn't know Mum and if they waited for Uncle Chris, she'd be getting hungry. "I'll do it," she muttered, shaking up the bottle. "It's OK, Mum. See you in a minute."

She hurried out to the garden where Dapple was waiting eagerly by the gate, obviously watching out for her bottle.

"Hey," Lola murmured. "Go back from the gate a bit, sweetheart." She shooed Dapple gently so she could get in and then held out the bottle. "Look, I've got it. Come on." She leaned over Dapple the way Uncle Chris had shown her – if Dapple was feeding from her mum, she'd have her mum's body above her. Leaning over was meant to make the bottle-feeding seem a little more natural.

Dapple sucked greedily at the bottle – she'd got so good at it now, it usually only took a couple of minutes for her to drink it all. Lola had worried that maybe they weren't giving her enough since she was finishing the milk so quickly but Uncle Chris promised that it was OK. He said that fawns weren't good at knowing how much was enough – given a chance, they'd drink way too much and make themselves ill. So it was better to stick with the measured amount of milk, even if Dapple did make starved faces when she'd finished.

Lola sniffed again and Dapple stopped sucking for a moment and looked up at her. "Sorry," Lola murmured. "It's OK. Keep going."

But Dapple didn't go back to her bottle. She let go and gazed up at Lola. And then

she reached up and licked Lola's cheek – a
slobbery, milky, lovely lick that made Lola cry
even more.

Lola was extra glad that she had Dapple to care
for over the summer holidays. Lola had told
Uncle Chris he didn't need to do any of the
feeds now she wasn't at school – she was glad of
the extra work. She'd been hoping to meet up
with Paige while they were off school – maybe
with Maisie and Hannah too. But after Mum
had called Paige's mum and explained that Lola
wouldn't be able to make it to Paige's birthday
sleepover, all that was off. If it hadn't been for
the fawn, Lola would have been even more
miserable. It was amazing to watch Dapple
grow so fast, though, and to know that it was

partly because she was looking after her.

Lola started to understand what Uncle Chris had meant about the two and a half metre fences for keeping deer out of gardens. She'd definitely caught Dapple giving the fence around her little run some thoughtful looks.

"I think she needs more space," she told Uncle Chris when he next came over to check up on Dapple.

"Mmmm." Uncle Chris looked around the run. "I think you're right. What about taking her for a walk round the garden before you feed her?"

Lola looked surprised. "Will we have to put her on a lead? Won't she run off?"

"Not if she hasn't had her milk," Uncle Chris pointed out. "If she wanders too far, you can just bring out her bottle. She'll come straight back."

"If you're sure…" Lola said. "Yeah! She's going to love getting to explore the garden."

"Just don't let her go near the football net!" Mum called from the kitchen.

That afternoon, Lola got Dapple's bottle ready and brought it out to the garden with her. She put it down in a clump of long grass growing next to the gate of the run and then unlatched the gate. Dapple surged eagerly forward, nearly tripping Lola over and nudging at her for the milk. But Lola stepped away from the run, beckoning the little deer out into the garden, and Dapple followed after her, ears twitching curiously.

Lola wondered how much she remembered of her days with her mother. She must have walked this way so many times, pattering after her mother as they searched for a safe hiding place for Dapple to wait away the day. But now the fawn seemed only excited, hopping and springing about, and taking short little dashes across the grass. She seemed to be testing out how big the space really was after being shut up in the run.

Lola watched her, giggling as the fawn bounced but feeling sad too. Until now she hadn't realized just how small Dapple's run was. She had been proud of how well they were looking after her and she'd been quite sure the fawn was happy. But seeing her loving the freedom of the garden changed that.

"It's OK," she whispered. "It won't be long before you're big enough to live out here all the time." She stopped as Dapple sniffed at a rose bush and then nibbled curiously at one of the flowers. What would it be like, not having to dash out every morning with a bottle? Lola wouldn't have to stand there laughing to herself as the fawn snorted and slobbered her way through her milk. Everything would be just like it was before – but somehow it was hard to imagine. Letting Dapple out to explore the garden felt like the first step to saying goodbye.

"I'll miss you," Lola murmured.

Lola didn't really mind that she wasn't going on a summer holiday this year. She went to stay with Dad for a long weekend in the middle of August and they went to a theme park, which was good because she and Dad both liked rollercoasters, and her mum really didn't – and she ate lots of pancakes, which were her favourite thing and something Dad was very good at cooking. She went over to Amie's house with Eloise too.

But she missed Mum and worried about Dapple, even though she knew Uncle Chris was looking after the fawn. It was weird, being back close to her old house and her old school, but staying in Dad's flat instead. Even though she loved spending time with Dad, Lola was glad to get back home – it *was* home now, she realized, with a little jolt of surprise. It really was.

When Dad dropped her off she took him into the garden to show him Dapple – very carefully. If they stood just by the big rose bush that Dapple thought was so delicious, then they could peer round at the fawn without her noticing them.

"She's so little!" Dad murmured and Lola shook her head.

"She isn't! She's grown loads. She actually looks bigger than when I last saw her on Thursday, Dad, honestly."

"You're obviously doing a really good job looking after her. She's amazing, Lola, I'm so glad you showed me. Look, I'd better get back now. See you soon, OK?"

"Do you want a snack, Lola?" Mum asked as Lola came back from waving Dad off.

"Mmm, can I have a bit of toast, please?" Then Lola frowned as she spotted a piece of paper on the table. It was folded in half and had her name on it. "What's that?"

"It's from Paige," Mum said, eyeing Lola a

little worriedly as if she wasn't sure how Lola was going to react. "She came round with her mum on Sunday afternoon. She didn't know you were away, of course. And then this note came through the letter box. You don't have to open it," she added.

Lola gave her a surprised look.

"If she's still upset with you, I mean. Although she didn't seem to be, when she came round."

"Oh." Lola picked up the note and unfolded it slowly. She was almost sure that Paige wouldn't write her a mean note – she wasn't that sort of person. But Paige had been so cross with her before.

Hi Lola

I'm sorry I was so angry about the fawn. I didn't understand why you couldn't have just told me. I was still upset with you but I talked to my mum

a couple of days ago, and she said you were right.
She's looked after fawns and other baby wild
animals before. She said they have to stay wild and
not get used to meeting people. (I still wish you'd told
me that – I wouldn't have minded.)
Sorry you're not here, I wanted to say hello. And I
wish you had come to my party.
Paige xx

"Is it all right?" Mum asked.

Lola nodded, smiling. "Her mum works at the same shelter as Uncle Chris. She told Paige he was right about not letting people visit the fawn."

"Oh, good. I did tell her mum that I'd ring her when you got back. Paige and Immy are at holiday club this week, but maybe Paige could come round afterwards?"

"Really?" Lola gripped the note tight. "Yes!

Can you call her now?"

"I can leave a message. Lola, stop jumping,
I'll drop the phone!"

Later that afternoon, Lola answered the door,
her heart thudding. What was Paige going to
say?

But in the end, her friend didn't say anything.
She just stared at Lola and then gave her a
massive hug. Then she yelped and handed Lola
a plastic bag that had been squashed between
them. "I forgot about it! Mum said Dapple
would like these. I hope they're still OK."

Lola looked into it, and laughed – the bag
was full of dandelions, the fat yellow flowers
looking fresh and crunchy. "She'll love them.
Do you want to see her now?"

"Can I?"

"I take her out in the garden before I feed her so she gets to explore more," Lola explained. "If you don't mind staying inside you can see her from the kitchen window. Or my bedroom – you'd see her really well from there. I just have to mix up her milk."

"How many times a day do you feed her?" Paige asked, watching as Lola poured the water on to the milk powder.

"Four times. But Uncle Chris does the

lunchtime feed when I'm at school. And he fed
her the whole time I was at Dad's. We reckon
she might be able to go down to three feeds a
day soon. She's grazing more when we take her
out of the run. OK, this is ready." She smiled
shyly at Paige. "I can't wait for you to see her
at last."

"Me too!"

Lola opened the gate of the run and Dapple
dashed out to check on the rose bush to see
if there were any new buds to eat. Mum had
told Lola that she'd given up hope of seeing
any roses that summer. Dapple ate all the
low-down ones and the other deer came and
nibbled away the higher buds.

"Here, Paige brought you a present," Lola
told her, pulling a handful of dandelions out
of the bag. She looked up at her window and

waved at Paige. She could see her friend's nose practically squished against the glass, watching as Dapple eagerly gobbled the flowers. There were so many that the fawn's muzzle was stained yellow with tiny glowing petals.

10

Lola pulled her school cardigan tightly round her as she slipped out of the side door. The mornings were definitely colder now that it was September, and the leaves were just starting to turn brown. Under the horse chestnut tree the deer lifted their heads and eyed her cautiously but they didn't race away. It made Lola glow inside that they knew her now. They knew they were safe.

There was a faint clanging from the run as Dapple stood up against the metal gate, clearly wondering why Lola was being so slow. Lola hurried round to the shed and slipped into the pen. "I can't take you out now," she said gently to the fawn. "School starts again today. I have to go soon. But I promise I'll let you explore this afternoon." She held up the bottle temptingly and Dapple grabbed at it.

Lola stood leaning over her, watching as she drank. Dapple was so much bigger now – Lola definitely didn't need to lean down as far. The fawn's white spots and dark stripes were fading too so she was more of a golden brown colour all over. She was beginning to look like the older deer, Lola realized, glancing back at the gathering under the horse chestnut tree.

Her stomach twisted a little. Soon Dapple would be old enough to leave the run and live in the wild again. Uncle Chris had already cut out her lunchtime feed because she was

grazing more. He said it
wouldn't be that long before
she didn't need milk at all –
before she didn't need *them*
at all.

"Got to go," Lola
whispered, as Dapple
slurped the last drops
out of the bottle. "I'd
better not make
Mum late on
the first day of
term. See you
this afternoon,
sweetheart."

She looked over her shoulder as she took
the bottle back to the kitchen. Dapple was
standing by the gate, watching her go.

"She's not a pet," Lola whispered to herself. "I always knew that." But it was so hard to imagine that one day soon she'd be coming home from school and Dapple wouldn't be there waiting for her.

"Do you want to come over for tea tomorrow?" Paige asked, catching up with Lola as she walked into school on the Monday morning just before half-term. "Mum said I could invite Maisie and Hannah too."

Lola shook her head. "I'm not sure I can. Sorry, Paige. Uncle Chris is coming to ours. He says he wants to have a look at Dapple."

Paige frowned. "Why?"

"I'm not sure." Lola sighed. "I think he's

going to say she's old enough to be out in the wild. It's nearly the end of October – that's when he said she'd be ready."

"Don't you think so?" Paige asked sympathetically.

"I suppose… But I can't imagine not having her…"

"Dapple's so lucky you found her," Paige pointed out, giving Lola a hug. "She really is. It'll be OK." She sighed. "Have you done that maths homework? I don't understand division the way Mr Marshall showed us. I wish we still had Miss Addison. Year Six is just too much hard work…"

Lola stood by the gate to the run, looking worriedly at Uncle Chris. "Do you really think she's old enough?" she asked again.

"Dapple's five months old now – at least. She might even be a little older. She's not taking bottles any more," Uncle Chris said gently. "When you let her out she's only coming back to the run out of habit. She could disappear into the wild bit of the garden or the cemetery any time she wanted to."

"But … but if she's coming back to the run without me waving a bottle at her, doesn't that mean she likes it?" Lola argued. And then she stopped, her shoulders drooping. "We don't want her to like it, do we?"

"Yeah. I know it's hard." Uncle Chris put his arm round her shoulders. "But I think she's ready."

"I know that really," Lola muttered. "I just don't want to do it."

"She's been calling to the other deer, hasn't she?" Uncle Chris reminded her. "She wants to be with them."

Lola nodded. She had seen at least one of the other deer nose-to-nose with Dapple through the wire fence – a young one, not that much bigger than Dapple herself. She unlatched the metal gate and pulled it wide open. Uncle Chris took a bit of string out of his pocket and tied the gate back against the fence so that it couldn't blow shut. Then they backed away into the garden, leaving a clear path for Dapple to come past them.

The fawn stepped eagerly out into the garden, her ears twitching as she eyed the pigeons on the fence and a squirrel bolting across the grass to the horse chestnut tree.

She doesn't know, Lola realized, as Dapple pottered happily around the bushes and stopped to eat a dandelion. *She doesn't know that this is it. We aren't going to call her back. She's free now and she doesn't understand.*

When Uncle Chris left to go back to the shelter, Lola climbed the ladder to the tree house and watched Dapple for the rest of the afternoon. Mum brought her some hot chocolate, but most of the time she was on her own. As the light began to fade, around five o'clock, she could see that Dapple was confused. She wandered about aimlessly, as if she didn't know what she was supposed to do. After all, how would she know?

Lola made herself stay still – she wanted so much to hurry down the ladder and lead the deer back to her shed. But in the end she didn't need to. Dapple gave one last look around the darkening garden and then padded through the grass and into the shed by herself.

Lola clambered down the ladder and dashed into the house to tell Mum and call Uncle Chris.

"She didn't go!" she yelped at him as soon as he answered the phone. "She's back in the shed."

"I did wonder if it would take her a while to work out what's going on," Uncle Chris said thoughtfully.

"Should I shut the gate again?" Lola asked, looking round at her mum. "Mum said what about foxes?"

"A fox might have tried to attack her when she was little but these days Dapple could give them a pretty serious kick. No, leave it open. She needs to understand that she can come and go as she pleases. Eventually she'll go. We hope. She needs to be a wild deer again, Lola. You know that."

"Yes." Even though he was on the other end of the phone, Lola tucked her hand behind her back so Uncle Chris couldn't see her crossing her fingers. Perhaps Dapple would stay forever?

Dapple continued to sleep in the shed but

each day she went gradually further and further from her safe little run. Lola spent the October half-term holiday mostly in the tree house, watching out for Dapple with a pair of binoculars that Uncle Chris had lent her. She held her breath when the fawn first stepped cautiously through the broken fence to the cemetery – she looked so small amidst the great expanse of grass and gravestones.

Lola wasn't sure that Dapple would come back that day. The fawn slipped away into the trees in the cemetery and Lola couldn't see her even with the binoculars. She watched for a while longer, scanning across the grass for a little golden brown deer, but there were only dogs, and a squirrel or two. She was sure that this was goodbye.

But then at bedtime she went out into the

garden. Even though she knew Dapple wouldn't be there, it was still a habit, going out last thing. Lola shone the torch around the empty run and then jumped as a velvet-soft nose pressed against her hand. Dapple nudged her gently and padded back to her basket in the shed.

Paige came over on the last day of half-term and they watched together, up in the tree house as they nibbled on a batch of cupcakes that Lola's mum had let them bake.

"Do you think she'll keep coming back here to sleep, then?" Paige asked, fiddling with the focus on the binoculars.

"I don't know – I sort of hope so but I shouldn't." Lola sighed. "Roe deer are supposed to be active through the night, not just in the daytime. Staying in the shed at night isn't a very deer-like thing to do."

"Can they see in the dark?" Paige asked, surprised.

"Uh-huh. I looked it up. They see loads better than we do. They've got horizontal pupils that let in a lot of light. And they have a reflector at the back of their eyes that we don't have as well – that helps. You know when cats' eyes glow in the dark sometimes? It's because they have it too. Look! There she is, coming back towards the fence."

Paige peered eagerly through the binoculars. "Wow. Are you sure that's her, Lola? She's so big."

"Yeah, she's a lot darker than the other deer who come into the garden. She had dark stripes on her back when she was tiny and now she's almost black – that's her winter coat."

Paige kept watching and Lola gazed at the fence and the blackberry bushes, waiting for Dapple to pop through into the garden. But she didn't appear.

"Oh, I think she's gone away again," Paige reported. "I'm pretty sure that was her darting off. Although there's another couple of deer moving about in the trees. This is such a cool place, Lola, this tree house."

"I know. I really want to sleep out here but

I think it might be too spooky in the middle of
the night."

"Would your mum let you?" Paige asked.

"She said I could, but I'd have to use my
sleeping bag and my duvet and extra blankets,
because it would be so cold. I don't think I'd
mind the cold, though. It just might be a bit
weird on my own…"

"I could come over," Paige suggested, fiddling
with the binoculars again so as not to look at
Lola. *As if she isn't sure I'd say yes,* Lola realized
at last.

"That would be amazing," she said. "Are you
sure you wouldn't be scared up here? It'd be
really dark."

"I've got a torch." Paige looked around
the tree house excitedly. "I'd love to sleep
up here." Then she sighed. "I can hear my

mum talking to yours, she's come to pick me up. Let's go and ask when we can have our sleepover."

That night, for the first time, Dapple wasn't around the shed and the run when Lola came to look for her at bedtime. But she'd been coming back later and later and Lola wasn't too worried. Or at least, she tried to tell herself she wasn't. As she got ready for bed she kept stopping to peer out of the window. It was far too dark to see Dapple slipping back through the garden but Lola kept looking.

She woke up in the morning to a heavy frost patterning the window and she wrapped a thick hoodie over her pyjamas before she hurried outside. The grass was frosted, each blade coated in ice that crunched as she walked across it to the shed.

The Hideaway Deer

"Dapple?" she murmured. But the shed and the run were so still and quiet, Lola knew that the little deer wasn't there. She had gone at last.

"Lola... Are you awake?"

Lola blinked and wriggled. She felt stiff and her nose was cold. She wondered for a moment if she'd left her bedroom window open but then she remembered – it was Paige calling her. They were up in the tree house.

It had taken a while to persuade Paige's mum – she wasn't worried that it would be too cold to sleep out, or not that worried at least, but she was afraid that Paige would somehow manage to fall out of the tree in the middle of the night. And then Lola had been due for a weekend at her dad's so it was late November before they managed to have their tree house sleepover. Lola had kept on watching out for Dapple and she was almost sure she'd seen her once out in the garden after school. But only almost.

"Yes, I'm awake. Are you?" Lola said. She was too sleepy to think straight. Of course Paige was awake, if she was talking. "Do you want to get up? It's getting light. It must be about half past seven."

"Are you hungry? I'm really hungry." There was a shuffling noise as Paige wriggled around in her sleeping bag and then a crunch. "I found the popcorn!"

"Let's go and sit outside and eat it." Lola scrabbled about for her hat and then stood up in her sleeping bag like a caterpillar. She shuffled to the door and pulled it open and they curled up on the little front platform of the tree house, gazing at the misty garden and the cemetery beyond.

Paige passed Lola the bag of popcorn her

mum had let her bring for a midnight feast (it
had been more like a quarter-past-ten feast in
the end) and they sat munching slowly.

Lola was still half asleep so it took her a little
while to realize what she was seeing – and then
she nudged Paige with her elbow. "Look!" she
whispered.

Padding out from between the brambles
was a line of deer, their grey-brown coats half
disappearing into the mist. They came slowly
into the garden, stopping here and there to
graze – and at the very end of the line was a
small one, grey-brown along her sides like the
others but her back was almost black.

Lola stared.

"Is that her?" Paige breathed, her hand
halfway into the popcorn. "Is it, Lola? The one
at the end?"

The deer looked up with a mouthful of frosted grass, peering at them thoughtfully. Lola knew that she probably couldn't see them from that far away or at least not very well. But it felt as if Dapple was gazing straight at them. She looked so dark and sleek – so perfect.

"Yes," she whispered to Paige. "She came back. That's my Dapple."